Dip the brush into water, then brush it across the black patterns and lines within each shape to see the paint magically appear.

Wash the brush before you start to paint each new shape, and use the flap at the back of the book to stop the paint from seeping through to the next page.

Usborne

Rainforest
Magic Painting
Book

Illustrated by
Marcella Grassi

Designed by
Alice Reese